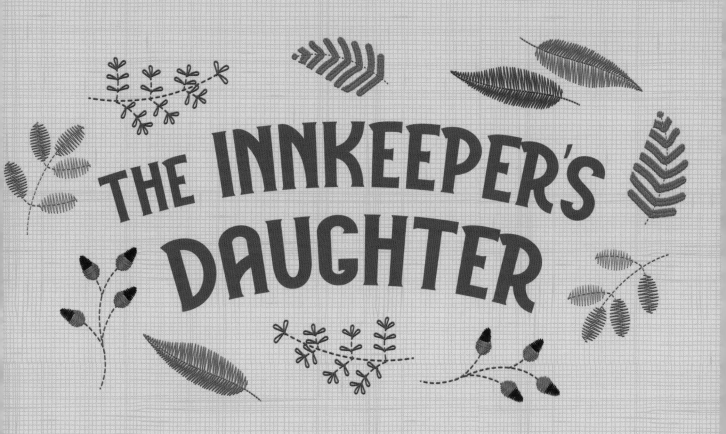

THE INNKEEPER'S DAUGHTER

To my sisters.
Thank you for being my wings
when I'm too tired to fly.

–Calie

Text © 2022 Calie Schmidt
Illustrations © 2022 Alexandra Sanches
All rights reserved.

This is not an official publication of the Church of Jesus Christ of Latter-day Saints. The opinions and views expressed herein belong solely to the author and do not necessarily represent the opinions or views of Cedar Fort, Inc. Permission for the use of sources, graphics, and photos is also solely the responsibility of the author.

ISBN 13: 978-1-4621-3817-3

Published by CFI, an imprint of Cedar Fort, Inc.
2373 W. 700 S., Suite 100, Springville, UT 84663
Distributed by Cedar Fort, Inc., www.cedarfort.com

Library of Congress Control Number: 2022943194

Cover design and interior layout by Shawnda T. Craig
Cover design © 2022 Cedar Fort, Inc.

Printed in the United States of America

10 9 8 7 6 5 4 3 2 1

Printed on acid-free paper

THE INNKEEPER'S DAUGHTER

CFI • An imprint of Cedar Fort, Inc.
Springville, Utah

written by Calie Schmidt

illustrated by Alexandra Sanches

A LONG TIME AGO,

in a small Hebrew city,
lived an innkeeper's daughter
so young, sweet, and pretty.

Each morning she'd wake
well before dawn
to take care of the travelers
until they moved on.

Wash clothes, cook meals,
chop wood, start the fire.
Each day, so much work.
Each night, deeply tired.

And if she found
a free moment to spare,
she'd sit in the corner,
embroidering with care.

Fine needle work she
learned from her mother
who passed away leaving young
girls with their father.

The innkeeper's daughter,
the first sister born,
worked hard to give care
to her family and home.

She loved her sweet sisters
and hardworking father.
Vowed always to help and
tried never to bother.

Travelers were many,
The streets were a bustle.
The marketplace filled with
excitement and hustle.

Great booths were put up.
More than ever before.
Instruments, spices, nuts—
and much more!

As she viewed the shops,
one place caught her eye.
Rainbows of cloth
made her heart want to fly.

Such beautiful colors!
Such beautiful wraps,
but all she could pay for
was plain muslim scraps.

Though simple and plain,
the scraps had potential.
She brought them straight home.
Took care to be gentle.

Every free moment
she had before bed
was spent with a frame,
a needle, and thread.

As the days passed by,
the work became more.
Each minute, each second,
another big chore.

At night, by a candle,
with needle and thread,
beautiful patterns
blossomed and spread.

Patiently stitching from
memories sweetly.
Her mother's designs, through
her own hands, flowed neatly.

The time to pay taxes,
the census was now.
The inn became crowded.
No place to sit down.

A knock at the door,
so soft and so faint.
There stood on the threshold
a couple so quaint.

Traveling light, their
possessions were few.
The woman, with child,
any time now was due.

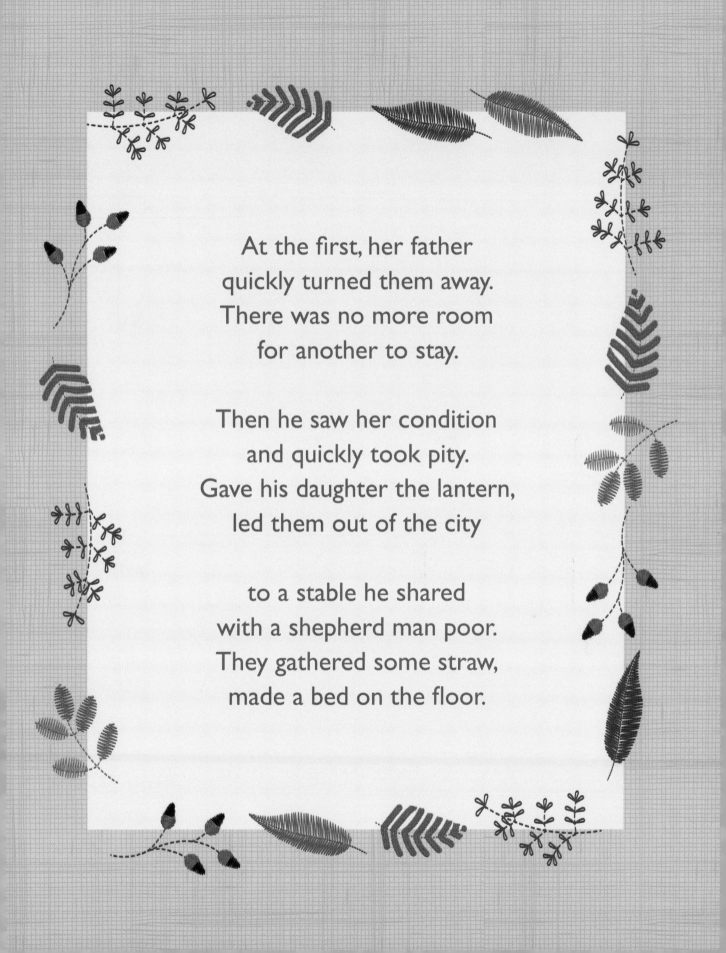

At the first, her father
quickly turned them away.
There was no more room
for another to stay.

Then he saw her condition
and quickly took pity.
Gave his daughter the lantern,
led them out of the city

to a stable he shared
with a shepherd man poor.
They gathered some straw,
made a bed on the floor.

The time came for the
inn keeper's daughter to leave.
She pulled out the needlework
tucked in her sleeve.

Approaching the woman
who lay on the hay,
she gave her the cloth
and softly did say,

"My heart has gone into
this linen so small.
I know it's not much,
but I gave it my all.

Please take this tonight.
Your babe will come soon."
Then leaving her gift,
she returned to her room.

Still awake, working late
into the dark night.
In through the window
a new star beamed bright.

This light was unlike
any other she'd seen.
Glorious! Magnificent!
Created for a King.

She remembered some men.
Were they prophet or beggar?
Telling of a star and
a new righteous Savior.

Was this the Messiah
that had been foretold
by those men at the temple
and prophets of old?

First she turned to her sisters.
Oh good, they're still sleeping.
Tucked them in tight,
taking care of their keeping.

Then crept down the stairs.
The inn was so soundless,
the silent town sleeping,
the sky clear and cloudless.

Allowed the bright star
to light up her way
on the same path she
followed earlier that day.

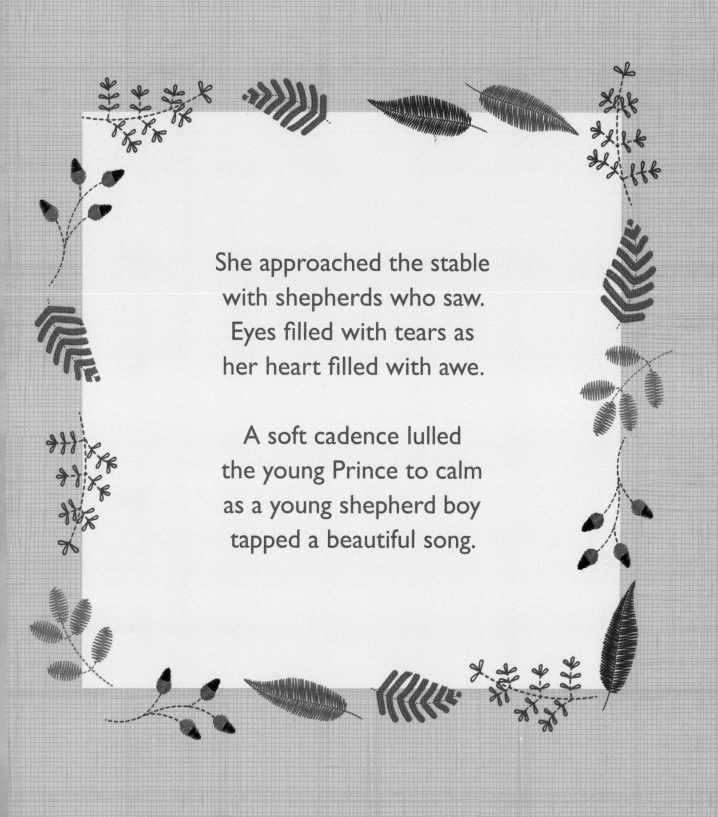

She approached the stable
with shepherds who saw.
Eyes filled with tears as
her heart filled with awe.

A soft cadence lulled
the young Prince to calm
as a young shepherd boy
tapped a beautiful song.

Then saw swaddled tight
in a small scrap un-dyed,
embroidered designs tucked
around the babe's side.

Mary, seeing the girl
through the crowd in a part,
mouthed a silent "thank you"
with her hand on her heart.

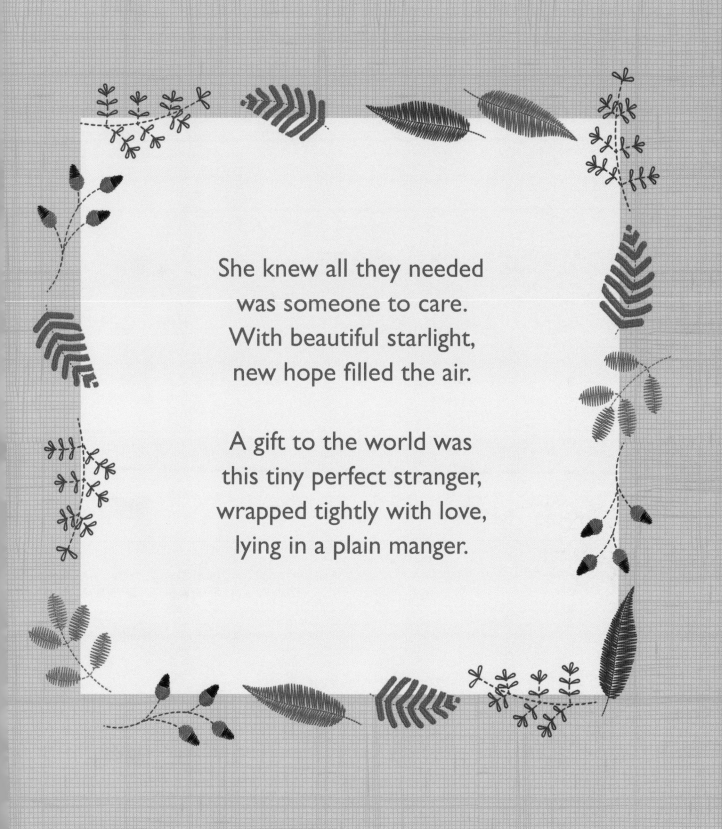

She knew all they needed
was someone to care.
With beautiful starlight,
new hope filled the air.

A gift to the world was
this tiny perfect stranger,
wrapped tightly with love,
lying in a plain manger.

THE END